Life with

Dick and Jane

A N D   F R I E N D S

Dick and Jane® is a registered trademark of Addison-Wesley Educational Publishers, Inc.
Text and illustrations from NOW WE READ, copyright © 1965 by Scott, Foresman and Company, copyright renewed 1993;
THE NEW GUESS WHO, copyright © 1965 by Scott, Foresman and Company, copyright renewed 1993.

From BEFORE WE READ. Illustrations copyright © 1951 by Scott, Foresman and Company.
From WE READ MORE PICTURES. Illustrations copyright © 1965 by Scott, Foresman and Company,
copyright renewed 1979. Text copyright © 2004 Pearson Education, Inc.

Published by Grosset & Dunlap, a division of Penguin Young Readers Group,
345 Hudson Street, New York, New York 10014.
GROSSET & DUNLAP is a trademark of Penguin Random House LLC.
Printed in China

ISBN 978-0-448-43823-8   10 9 8 7 6 5 4 3 2

CONTENTS

CONTENTS

Who Wants to Ride?

"Oh, Father," said Dick.
"Do you want the car?"

"I do," said Father.

Jane said, "Sally! Sally!
Father wants the car.
Come and help Dick and me."

"Sally! Sally!" said Dick.
"Will you come and help?"

Father said, "I will help you.
Sally is in the house."

"Who wants to go with me?
Who wants a ride?"

"Not I!" said Dick.
"Not I!" said Jane.

"Tim and I do," said Sally.
"We will go for a ride."

A Book for Sally

Mother said, "Look here, Sally.
See the house in here.
Do you like this book?"

"No, Mother," said Sally.
"I do not like that book.
I will find a book for me.
Jane will like that one.
We can get that one for Jane."

"Cars," said Mother.
"I see cars and cars and cars.
Dick will like this book.
We will get this one for Dick."

Sally said, "Oh, oh!
See who is in this book.
Here is Tim!
Here is Tim in a book.
This is the book I like.
This is the book for me!"

Look Here

Jane said, "Is Sally here?"

"Who wants Sally?" said Dick.

"I do," said Jane.
"I can not find Sally.
Get up, Dick.
Get up and help me find Sally."

"Sally is here," said Dick.

Jane said, "No, Dick, no!
Sally is not in this house.
Get up and do something, Dick!
Help me find Sally."

"Oh, Jane," said Dick.
"You can find Sally."

"Look here, Jane!" said Sally.
"You can find Tim and me.
Come and see what we can do.
Tim can do something for me.
And I can do something for Dick.
Come and see what we can do."

Get the Ball In

"No, no, Dick!" said Father.
"Do not look down at the ball.
You want it to go up here.
Look up here, Dick."

"I did look up," said Dick.
"But the ball did not go up."

Father said, "Go get the ball.
We will see what I can do with it."

"Look at that!" said Father.
"See what I did with the ball."

Dick said, "It did go up.
But it did not go in.
I will go up and get it."

"Look here," said Dick.

"I can do something with the ball.

I can get it in here now.

It did not go up and in.

But it will go down and in."

See It Work

"Look at that!" said Dick.
"See it come up."

Jane said, "Look, Sally.
See it work."

Sally said, "I see it work.
But I do not like it.
I want it to go down now.
I do not want it to get me."

"Oh, Sally," said Father.
"It will not get you."

Sally said, "Look at Tim!
Jump down, Father, jump down.
Get my Tim for me."

Father said, "I can not get Tim.
I want to help you, Sally.
But I can not jump down."

Dick said, "Look, Sally.
It can work for you.
It can get Tim!"

"I see it," said Sally.
"I see it work for me.
Up it comes with my little Tim."

The Dog for Dick

Father said, "Come with me.
I want to get something for Spot."

"Oh, Father," said Dick.
"We want to look at the dogs now."

Jane said, "Look at this little dog!
It wants to play with us."

Sally said, "Jump, little dog.
Jump! Jump! Jump!
We like you."

Dick said, "Down, Spot, down.
I want to see the little dogs."

Dick said, "Look here, Father.
This little dog likes us.
And we like it.
Will you get it for us?"

Father said, "You have a dog.
What will you do with Spot?
Do you want Spot to go away?"

Jane said, "Look at Spot!
Spot wants to run away now."

Dick said, "Oh, Spot!
I like that little dog.
But I do not want it.
I want my dog!
I want you!"

Guess What It Is

Jane said, "I have something.

It is something for us.

Can you guess what it is?

Who wants to guess?"

Sally said, "I want to guess.
Can it run and jump?
Can it play with us?"

Jane said, "No, Sally.
It can not run and jump.
It can not play with us.
But we can play with it."

Dick said, "Now I want to guess.

It is red.

It is a red ball.

You have a red ball for us."

Jane said, "Oh, Dick.

You did guess what I have.

It is a red ball."

Sally said, "Oh, Jane.

Dick did not guess.

Dick can see what you have.

Look, Jane, look.

Dick can see the red ball.

Look at that!"

What Is This?

Jane said, "Come here, Dick.
Will you play with Puff and me?
Come and play ball with us."

Dick said, "I have work to do.
Come and help me with my work."

Jane said, "I can guess what this is.
It is a little house for Puff and me."

"No, no!" said Dick.
"This is not a house for you.
This is a car for me.
But you and Puff can ride in it.
Two can ride in my car."

"Oh my!" said Jane.
"Help! Help!"

Dick said, "Down, Spot!
Go away! Go away!
Three can not ride in my car."

Jane said, "Look, Dick!

That is not a car now.

I did guess what it is.

It is a little house.

It is a house for Spot and Puff!"

Fun for Three

Jane said, "We want to play.
What can we do to have fun?"

Mother said, "Help me do this.
And I will help you three have fun."

Mother said, "See what I have.

I have two for Dick and two for Jane.

And I have two for Sally."

Dick said, "I want two big ones."

Mother said, "No, Dick.

I have a big one for you.

I have a big one for Jane.

And I have a big one for Sally."

"This is not fun," said Sally.
"This is work.
Work! Work! Work!
I want to have fun."

"You will," said Mother.
"This big one is for you.
You will have fun now."

Father said, "One, two, three!
What do I see?"

Dick said, "Run, run, run!
Here we come."

Father said, "Oh, no!
Away I go!"

Dick and Father

Dick said, "This is fun.
Can you do this?"

"I can," said Father.
"But I do not want to do that."

Father said, "Look here, Dick.
Can you do this?"

"I can," said Dick.
"But I do not want to.
Not now!"

Father said, "What do you have?
Did you find something?"

Dick said, "Get down, Father.
Jump down and see what I have."

"See what I have!" said Dick.
"I have one, two, three."

"Oh my!" said Father.
"I see what you have.
And I see what I do not have."

Up and Down

Dick said, "One, two, three!
Down I go."

Jane said, "Now I will go down.

One, two, three!

Here I come.

This is fun."

Sally said, "Here I come, Jane.

I can come up, and I can go down."

Jane said, "Come down, Sally.
It is fun to come down.
We will help you."

"No, no, no," said Sally.
"I do not want to come down.
This is not fun for me.
I want my mother!
I want my father!"

Sally said, "One, two, three!
Down we come.
This is fun now."

Do Something Funny

Father said, "Come here, Dick.
Come here, Jane.
We have work to do now."

Sally said, "I want to play.
I want to do something funny."

Sally said, "Look at me.
Who do I look like?"

"I can guess," said Mother.
"You look like me."

Dick said, "What can we do, Jane?
Can we do something funny?"

Jane said, "Look at us.
Do Dick and I look funny?"

Sally said, "You do!
You do look funny."

Dick said, "Oh, Father.
Will you and Mother play with us?
Will you do something funny?"

Father said, "Look at us!
Do we look funny now?"

"Oh, oh, oh!" said Jane.
"What a funny father we have!
What a funny mother!"

A Funny House

Sally said, "What is that, Dick?"

Dick said, "Guess, Sally.
Guess what it is."

Sally said, "I can not guess.

Is it something for us?

Is it for Pam and Penny and me?"

Dick said, "No, Sally.

It is not for you three.

It is a little house.

But it is not a house for you."

Pam said, "A house!
What a funny house!
Who wants a house like that?"

"Come with me," said Dick.
"Come and see what I do with it.
You will see who wants it."

Dick said, "Look!

Look at the little house now.

Can you guess what it is for?"

"Now we can," said Penny.

"We can see who wants that house."

What Will We Get?

Dick said, "Come with me.
I will get something funny for us."

Jane said, "What will you get?
Will you get a book?"

"You will see," said Dick.
"You will like what I get."

"Look up, Jane," said Dick.

"That is what I want to get.

I will get three.

I will get two big ones for us.

I will get a little one for Sally."

Jane said, "I like the red one.

Get that funny red one for me."

Dick said, "Come, Sally.
We will go now."

"No, no," said Sally.
"I see something I want."

Jane said, "Oh, Dick.
I can guess what Sally wants.
Get one for Sally.
And get two for us."

"My, oh my!" said Mother.

"What do I see?

One, two, three!

You do not look like my three to me."

Guess Who

Sally said, "See my cars.

See my cars go up, up, up.

One, two, three.

Up go my three little red cars."

Father said, "Oh, Sally.

It is fun for you to play here.

But we have work to do.

Run and play with the red ball.

You can have fun with that."

Jane said, "Spot! Spot!

You can not play here.

Go away, Spot."

Dick said, "Come here, Father!
Come and see what Spot did."

Sally said, "Oh, Dick.
I can do that.
I can do what Spot did."

Sally said, "Look! Look!
I did something funny."

Jane said, "I want to do that.
Dick and I can do it."

Father said, "Here, Puff.
I will help you do it."

Dick said, "Look here, Mother.
See what we did.
Guess who this big one is."

"Guess who this is," said Jane.

"Guess who this is," said Sally.
"And see the two little ones.
Guess who! Guess who!"

Something Red

Mother said, "Here we go.
We can ride and play.
Who wants to play with me?"

"We do," said Dick and Jane.
"I do," said Sally.

Mother said, "I see something little.
Who can find something little?"

"I see a little house," said Jane.
"I see a little car," said Dick.

Sally said, "I can not see.
Get away, Jane.
I want to find something little."

Mother said, "I see something big.
Who can find something big now?"

"I see a big, big house," said Jane.
"I see a big car," said Dick.

Sally said, "I want to see.
Get away, Dick.
I want to find something big."

Father said, "I see a big dog.
Who can find it?"

"I see three little dogs," said Dick.
"But I can not find the big one."

"I want to see," said Sally.
"I want to see the three little dogs."

Mother said, "I see something red.
Who can find something red now?"

"I can!" said Sally.
"I see a red ball.
I see a red car and a red house.
I see a funny red dog.
Look here in my book.
You can find something red in here."

Go, Go, Go

Go, Dick, go.

Go, go, go.

Help, help!

Jane

Dick! Dick!
Look, Dick.

Oh, Dick!
Help Jane.
Go help Jane.

Go, Jane.

Go, Jane, go.

Puff

Oh, Dick.

Help Sally.

Dick, help Sally!

Puff! Puff!

Oh, Puff!

Look, Dick.

Look, Jane.

Look at Puff.

Help! Help!

Oh, look.

Look, Puff.

Look, Spot.

Help! Help!
Run, Spot!
Run, Spot, run!

Sally! Sally!
Look at me.
Look at Dick.

Jane and Puff

Jane said, "Here, Puff.
Come here."

"Look!" said Jane.
"Look here, Puff."

Jane said, "Puff! Puff!
Look at this.
Come here and look at this."

Come and Ride

Dick said, "Come here, Puff.
Come and ride with Spot."

"Oh, Dick," said Jane.

"Puff can ride with me."

Jane said, "Look, Dick.
Look at this.
Puff can ride with me.
Spot can ride with you.
Come and ride."

Look in Here

Mother said, "Come, Sally.
Come in here with me."

Sally said, "Oh, Mother!
Can you come here?
I want you to look at this."

Sally said, "Look in here, Mother.
Look at me
and me
and me!"

Look Here

Here, Spot.

Here, Spot.

Come here, Spot.

Come, Puff.
Come here, Puff.
Run, run, run.

Oh, Puff!
Oh, oh!
Look at me!

Tim

Oh, Mike.

Look at Sally.

Mike! Mike!

Come here.

Come here, Mike!

Help me!

Look at me.
Look at Tim.
Look at Tim go.

Mike

Oh, Sally.
Go get Tim.
Get Tim.

Go get Pam.

Sally, get Pam.

Run, Sally, run.

Dick! Jane!
Look at Penny.
Look at Pam.
Look at Tim.

Pam

Penny! Penny!
Come here.
Help me, Penny.
Get me down.

Mike! Mike!

Come here, Mike.

Come help Pam.

Help Pam get down.

Come, Pam.

Get down.

Get down, Pam.

Down, Down, Down

Down, Sally!

Get down.

Get down, Sally.

Down, Pam!
Down, Penny!
Get down, Pam.
Get down, Penny.

Jane! Jane!

Help me!

Help Pam.

Help Penny.

Jump, Jump, Jump

Jump, Tim.

Jump, Tim.

Jump, Tim, jump.

Penny! Penny!

Look at Sally.

Look at Tim.

Look at Sally jump.

Oh, Puff.
Jump down.
Jump, Puff, jump.

Look at Me

Oh, Dick!

Look at me.

Look at me, Mike.

Dick! Mike!

Get Spot.

Run, run, run.

Oh, get Spot.

Come, Spot.

Come here, Spot.

Mike! Pam! Penny!

Look at me.

Look at me, Jane.

Oh, look at me, Sally.

Will Spot Run Away?

Sally said, "I want to get Spot.
Spot will run away."

Dick said, "I can get Spot.
Spot will not run away."

Dick said, "Here, Spot!
Come and get this.
This is for you.
Run, Spot, run."

Sally said, "Is that for Spot?
I want that!"

Mother said, "Oh, Sally.
That one is for Spot.
Here is one for you.
And here is one for Dick."

Sally said, "Spot gets one.
Dick gets one.
And I get one!"

Here I Come

Mother said, "Dick! Dick!
Come in the house.
I want you to help Jane."

Dick said, "Here I come.
Mother wants me to help you."

"Look at that!" said Jane.
"That will not help me.
Go away, Dick, go away.
You can not come in the house."

"See me!" said Dick.
"I can do this.
Here I come!"

Sally and Dick

"Help, Sally, help!" said Dick.

Sally said, "Look, Dick, look.
Look at me."

"Look, Sally, look," said Dick.

"Look at me now."

Play Ball

"Sit, Spot, sit," said Dick.

"I want to play ball."

Father said, "Go, Dick, go.
Play ball."

"No, Spot, no," said Dick.

"I want to play ball with Father."

"Go away, Spot!"

Sally Helps

Sally can help.

Sally can help Mother.

Oh, no!

Sally can help.

Sally can help Mother.

Mother and Jane

Mother can sew.
Jane wants to sew.

Mother can sew.
Jane can sew.

Oh, no.

Silly, silly Jane.

Sally and Jane

Sally said, "What are you doing, Jane?
What are you doing with that bag?"

Jane said, "One, two, three!"

Sally did not jump.

Sally did not run away.

Spot jumped.

Spot ran away.

"Come, Spot, come," said Jane.

"Good Spot," said Sally.

Funny Pam

Mother wants shoes.

Pam wants shoes.

Funny, funny Pam.

Father

"Look, look," said Father.

"A ball."

"What can you do?" said Dick.
"What can you do with the ball?"
Father said, "I can kick the ball."

"I can kick the ball with my foot," said Father.

Funny, funny Father.

Mother Makes
Something

"Look!" says Mother.
"Look at what I have.
I will make something for you."

"Look!" says Jane.

"Look at me."

Oh, no!

Dick and Father

"I will help," said Dick.

"I will help you with the pigs."

"Oh, no!" said Dick.

"Look! Look at the pig!" said Dick.

Dick said, "I will help you.
I will help you, Father!"

At The Farm

Dick is at the farm.

Dick is at the farm with Grandfather.

Dick can help.

Dick can help Grandfather at the farm.

The dog can help, too!

Mike and Father

Mike and Father are in the park.
Mike buys popcorn.

Mike and Father are walking in the park.

"Look, Father, look," said Mike.

"Look at the plane."

Mike said, "Look, Father, look!
Look at the birds.
Look at my popcorn."

Dick and Jane

Dick can help.

Dick can help Jane.

Oh, no!

Who can help Dick?

Mother can help.

Mother can help Dick.